GRANDPA BEAR'S
FANTASTIC SCARF

WRITTEN AND ILLUSTRATED BY

GILLIAN HEAL

BEYOND
WORDS
Publishing
INC

Beyond Words Publishing, Inc.
4443 NE Airport Road
Hillsboro, Oregon 97124-6074
503-693-8700 / 1-800-284-9673

Editor: Michelle Roehm
Art direction and design: Connie Lightner

Printed in Hong Kong
Distributed to the book trade by Publishers Group West

Also by Gillian Heal: *The Halfpennys Find a Home*

Library of Congress Cataloging-in-Publication Data
Heal, Gillian.
    Grandpa Bear's fantastic scarf / written and illustrated by
Gillian Heal.
        p.   cm.
    Summary: A wise old bear teaches his grandson about how to
approach life and happiness, using the scarf he weaves each day as a
metaphor.
    ISBN 1-885223-41-2
    [1. Grandfathers — Fiction. 2. Bears — Fiction. 3. Scarves — Fiction.
4. Weaving — Fiction.]   I. Title.
PZ7.H3435Gr   1997
[Fic] — dc20   96-8543
                                                         CIP
                                                          AC

Remembering
Judith Karelitz—
maker of wonderful
kaleidoscopes
and a special friend

Grandpa Bear and the little bear sat on the porch step side by side, watching for the evening star.

It was chilly, so Grandpa Bear wore his scarf. The little bear stroked it gently.

"I love your scarf," he said. "It's so long and cozy."

"It's like a part of me," said Grandpa Bear. "It grows long as my life grows long. I began to weave it when I was small like you."

The little bear
wanted to hear more.

"If you look carefully into my scarf, little bear, you'll see that there are two kinds of yarn. One goes **up** **a n d** **down** and the other goes **a c r o s s**.

The long up-and-down yarns are its bones. They shape the scarf—just as your bones and all you inherit from Ma and Pa and even from me shape you: likes, dislikes, loving berries, being afraid of bees, big paws . . ."

"I've got Pa's nose!" exclaimed the little bear. "Everyone says so!"

"There you are," said Grandpa Bear. "Your family passes on to you their ideas, fears, and joys . . . and even their noses! Each of these is a part of you, like the long, different-colored yarns holding your scarf together.

"It's important to check the colors of these yarns," he continued. "Perhaps an aunt gave you a bit of dull old yarn . . . like having grumpy mornings. Do you really want that in your scarf? You can't take it out of the days gone by; it's already woven in. But for the rest of your weaving, you want your own color. Choose your new color, tie it to the end of the old one, and keep going. No one says you have to live with someone else's handed-down color in your scarf. Make it your own."

The next day, the little bear looked closely at the weaving on Grandpa Bear's loom.

"Grandpa Bear, what are all those colors going across your up-and-down yarns?" he asked.

"Those are the other yarns. They are very special yarns, little bear, because *you* decide what they will be. You make your own magic with these yarns, with the colors you love, the colors of your life. And pretty soon you'll have yards of your own colors, just like me."

"YARDS!" cried the little bear. "That's LONG!"

"As long as my life," said the old bear.

The little bear thought what a **v e r y   l o n g   s c a r f** that would be.

Dreaming about colors and feeling rather
hungry with all this thinking, the little bear said
hopefully, "I like honey."

"There!" cried Grandpa Bear. "That's your first
color. Think of the color of honey!"

"I'd rather think," said the little bear, "about
the *taste* of honey. I'm EMPTY!"

So the two bears went to the kitchen to find a
little something to eat.

After lunch Grandpa Bear and the little bear went for a walk.

"Tell me more about weaving colors," said the little bear.

"What makes you happy?" asked Grandpa Bear.

"Apples!"

"Apples. Lots of colors in apples. R e d s , g r e e n s , o r a n g e , bits of **b r o w n ,** y e l l o w s . . ."

"And I like balloons and misty blue mountains and sunny days."

"Wonderful! I can see that your scarf is going to be bright. Now, if you were feeling sad or hurt, what color would you weave?"

"Dark, dark gray."

"That is a great color. So when you have a bad, gray, sad day, remember that it can be a beautiful color next to all the gorgeous apple colors and balloon colors."

The little bear gave a hop and a skip and a jump. He liked that idea.

"And then there is light and dark. Without light we would not know dark, and without dark we would not know light. Without cold we would not know how nice it is to be warm."

"Are there warm *colors*?" asked the little bear.

"Warm and cold colors. Can you think of a warm color?"

"FUR COLOR!"

The old bear laughed. "You are going to be a great weaver, little grandson!"

The two of them wandered on into their
favorite woods . . .

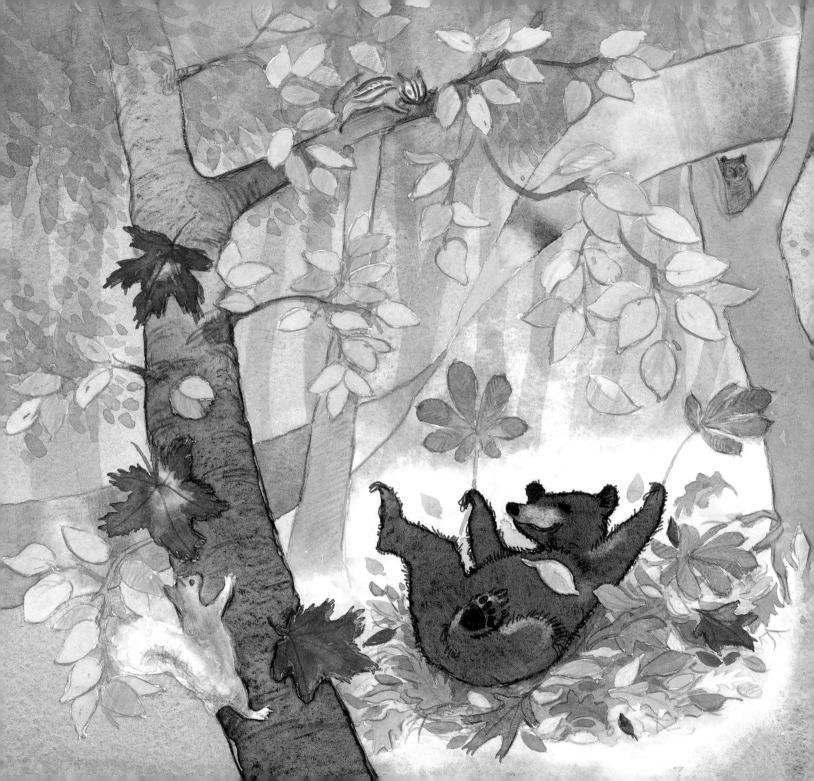

. . . where the little bear collected lots and lots
of beautiful leaves that were all different shapes
and colors.

Back home, Grandpa Bear began to weave at his big loom, and the little bear curled up in his scarf to watch.

"Look, Grandpa Bear, there's a sparkly bit of yarn here!"

"I weave each day, and some days are so **w o n d e r f u l** I use special yarn—fluffy or glittery. That's how I can remember the good days. One touch and I'm laughing!"

The little bear touched the sparkly bit, and he laughed too.

"Like life, weaving has good days and bad days. But happiness is something you make for yourself. It is your own responsibility."

The little bear looked very serious. "What do you mean, Grandpa Bear?"

"I mean, when you become a weaver, you shouldn't blame life or others for the dreary bit of weaving you make.

"Your weaving is your own. Check the up-and-down threads for strength. Change yarns if you want to. Change back if you make a mistake. Don't be afraid of change or of making mistakes, for they are part of learning to weave. Your scarf will be beautiful. You did it—you loved it and you made it.

"That, my little bear,
is making your own happiness."

Sitting on the porch step that evening,
Grandpa Bear wrapped the little bear up in part
of his long scarf.

The light dimmed and the two bears seemed
just one shape sitting so close together.

"I want to weave now too," said the little bear,
snuggling down beside Grandpa Bear.

"You shall," said the old bear. "Tomorrow we
will set up a loom just for you."

The stars came out in the dark, dark sky while
the little bear dreamed about weaving and colors
and his own adventure that would begin so soon.